THE
NEWEST
ADDAMS

"What do you think the baby will be?" asked Uncle Fester.

"I say it's a girl," said Wednesday.

"I say it's a boy," countered Pugsley.

"Girl!" snapped Wednesday.

"Boy!" her brother snarled back.

"Now, children," Granny cut in quickly. "Perhaps you're *both* right."

Before Wednesday or Pugsley could answer her, Gomez burst into the room. He was shaking with excitement. He threw his arms heavenward and struggled to speak.

"What news?" asked Granny eagerly.

"What *is* it?" asked Wednesday at the same time.

Gomez drew a long, long breath. "It's . . . an Addams," he said proudly.

Books by Ann Hodgman

My Babysitter Is a Vampire
My Babysitter Has Fangs
My Babysitter Bites Again
Stinky Stanley
Stinky Stanley Stinks Again

Available from MINSTREL Books

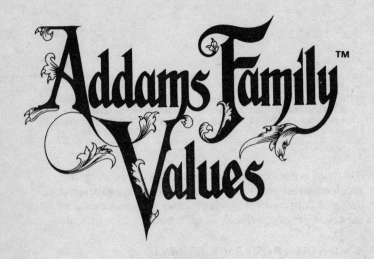

Addams Family™ Values

A NOVEL BY
ANN HODGMAN
FROM THE
SCREENPLAY
WRITTEN BY
PAUL RUDNICK
BASED ON THE
CHARACTERS
CREATED BY
CHARLES ADDAMS

A MINSTREL® BOOK

PUBLISHED BY POCKET BOOKS

New York   London   Toronto   Sydney   Tokyo   Singapore

This book is a work of fiction. Names, characters, places and incidents either are products of the author's imagination or are used fictitiously. Any resemblance to actual events or locales or persons, living or dead, is entirely coincidental.

A MINSTREL PAPERBACK *ORIGINAL*

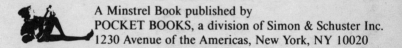 A Minstrel Book published by
POCKET BOOKS, a division of Simon & Schuster Inc.
1230 Avenue of the Americas, New York, NY 10020

Copyright © 1993 by Paramount Pictures

Cover artwork and photographs TM & Copyright © 1993 Paramount Pictures. All Rights Reserved.

ISBN: 0-671-88001-2

First Minstrel Books printing December 1993

10 9 8 7 6 5 4 3 2 1

A MINSTREL BOOK and colophon are registered trademarks of Simon & Schuster Inc.

Printed in the U.S.A.

CHAPTER ONE

THE NEWEST ADDAMS

*D*arkest midnight.

A wolf's howl ripped through the air as the full moon climbed slowly into the heavens. But the scene on which the moon cast its light was far from heavenly.

The air was draped in a foul, clammy fog. Fog wrapped itself around the decaying mansion imprisoned behind cruel iron gates. Fog curled around the faces of the hideous gargoyles on the roof. Fog wreathed the shrieking form of a bald-headed, hollow-eyed man standing on the roof itself—standing on the roof and howling at the full moon.

His name was Fester Addams.

Down below him, in a little cemetery, three people were digging a grave in the moonlight. One of the people was a boy—a stocky, squint-eyed kid who bore a distinct resemblance to an executioner. One was a white-faced, black-haired girl with a calmly murderous expression. And one was a dithery old grandma who seemed perfectly harmless—until you looked into her eyes.

The boy was Pugsley Addams. The girl was his sister, Wednesday. And the dithery old woman was their grandmother.

Granny's head was bowed in silent prayer. She cast a glance at the cardboard box Wednesday was holding and cleared her throat.

"Dearly beloved," she began, with a quaver in her voice.

A loud, angry meow interrupted her. It came from inside the cardboard box.

"Quiet," Wednesday ordered the box sternly. "We're not done."

In most families, of course, children don't go around digging graves at midnight. In most families, uncles don't scramble onto the roof at the first sight of the full moon. Most families don't pour boiling lead on Christmas carollers or keep a torture chamber in their basement, either. But the Addams family wasn't most families.

Take the Addams servants, for instance. Most families don't even *have* servants—much less a disembodied hand named Thing and a seven-foot-tall walking corpse named Lurch. Lurch was the Addams family butler. Thing was . . . well, Thing was useful when anyone needed a hand.

Right now Thing was inside wrestling with Gomez Addams, the children's father. (Hand-wrestling, of course.) Lurch was playing the organ. And elegant Morticia Addams, Gomez's wife, was watching the wrestling match while she knitted something small, black, and spidery.

Morticia put down her needles for a moment and gracefully folded her hands. "Gomez," she said, "I have marvelous news. I'm going to have a baby."

She paused.

"Right now," she added.

Granny patted Wednesday's hand. "It won't be long, dear," she said comfortingly. "The baby's sure to be here soon."

But to Wednesday and Pugsley, it seemed as though they'd already been waiting with Uncle Fester and Granny for hours. The hospital waiting room was too bright and cheerful for them. The vending machines didn't sell lizard roll-ups. They hadn't seen nearly enough accident victims being brought in on bloodied stretchers. Both children were getting bored and cranky.

"What do you think the baby will be?" asked Uncle Fester, trying to distract them.

"I say it's a girl," said Wednesday.

"I say it's a boy," countered Pugsley.

"Girl!" snapped Wednesday.

"Boy!" her brother snarled back.

"Now, children," Granny cut in quickly. "Perhaps you're *both* right!"

Before Wednesday or Pugsley could answer her, Gomez burst into the room. He was shaking with excitement. He threw his arms heavenward and struggled to speak.

"What news?" asked Granny eagerly.

"What *is* it?" asked Wednesday at the same time.

Gomez drew a long, long breath. "It's . . . an Addams," he said proudly.

Upstairs in the hospital nursery, little Pubert Addams was sleeping peacefully in his black bassinet. He had no idea that he was scaring the nurses half to death. Was it his looks? Like his father, Pubert had dead-white skin, jet-black hair parted down the middle, and a dark, pencil-thin mustache—not what you usually see on babies.

Or was it the fact that he already had the habit of throwing flaming arrows at anyone who tried to take him out of his bassinet?

Whatever it was, none of the nurses would go near little Pubert. But he was too young to notice. And since he was an Addams, it probably wouldn't have bothered him anyway.

When Pubert came home from the hospital, his nursery was all ready for him. Gomez had spent hours making the nursery just right, and now it was perfect for an Addams baby.

"It's an enchanting room," Morticia crooned, setting Pubert into his cradle and tucking a black satin sheet under his chin. "And you're an enchanting baby. So go to sleep."

But Pubert had other ideas. He started to scream at the top of his lungs.

"Oh, no, no," said Morticia gently. She picked up a teddy bear and pulled a string in its neck. The bear let out a murderous growl—and Pubert fell into a contented silence.

Then Gomez gave the baby's mobile a push. Glittering razor-sharp knives whirled around just inches from the baby's face. He stared at them in fascination and let out a happy coo.

"Welcome home, my son," said Gomez tenderly.

"How's the baby doing?" Fester stuck his head into the room. "Can I see him?" Without waiting for an answer, he rushed over to the cradle.

"He has my father's eyes," Gomez boasted.

"Gomez! Take them out of his mouth!" Morticia sounded shocked.

Fester reached in a scaly finger and chucked the baby under the chin. "Kitchy-kitchy-koo!" he said. "Hel-*lo,* baby! Look, he's got my finger! That's right, Pubert!"

A baby snarl floated up from the cradle as Fester tried to pull his finger back. And tried again. And finally yanked as hard as he could.

His finger was marked with the deep indentation of a tooth. Fester shook his head as he gazed at the wound. "Right down to the bone," he said fondly. "He's all Addams!"

None of the grown-ups noticed Wednesday and Pugsley standing in the doorway, forlorn and neglected.

"It's not true," Pugsley muttered to his sister.

"It is so," Wednesday whispered back. She was frowning as she stared at the adults bustling around the cradle. *"Everyone* knows it. When you have a new baby, one of the other children has to die."

Pugsley gulped. "Really?" he choked out.

His sister nodded. "It's a tradition. One of us has to go."

"Which one?" said Pugsley.

Wednesday turned and looked at him for a moment.

"Well," she finally replied, "they only need one boy."

CHAPTER TWO

ADJUSTING
TO
PUBERT

A hideous smell filled the Addams kitchen as Granny began to stir her cauldron. She dipped her spoon into the greenish mess and tasted it carefully. Then she shook her head and tossed in a handful of dead insects. With a puff of stinky steam, the greenish mess turned into a grayish mess. Granny smiled. *Much* better.

Little Pubert had been home for two weeks now, and life in the Addams household was pretty much back to normal. On this particular morning, Lurch was stoking the stove for Granny. Thing was out in the yard mowing the lawn with an antique scythe. Gomez and Uncle Fester were taking a fencing lesson. (They had already stabbed their instructor four times.) Morticia was making a poison-ivy wreath for the front door.

And Wednesday and Pugsley were helping out the best they could.

The two of them marched into the kitchen. "Granny," Wednesday announced, "we're going to give the baby a bath."

Granny gave her a demented smile. "Isn't that sweet?" she said. "But you don't need to wear rubber gloves to bathe a—"

"Where's the bleach?" Wednesday interrupted.

Bleach, of course, isn't exactly a No More Tears cleansing product. Maybe it would be more accurate to say that Wednesday and Pugsley were helping out the best they could—by trying to rid the world of Pubert Addams.

It wasn't fair. That's what they both thought. It wasn't fair for Pubert to get so much attention. All he could do was eat, cry, throw those stupid flaming arrows, and catch bats with his teeth. (Unlike most newborns, Pubert had a full set of teeth—pointed ones.) Stupid kiddie tricks—and yet the grown-ups in the family acted as though Pubert had invented dynamite!

Besides, no one had time for Wednesday and Pugsley now that Pubert was around. Morticia didn't notice when Wednesday learned how to French-braid her fingers. Gomez never said a word when Pugsley created an antidote to the smallpox vaccine.

"We could set fire to the house," Pugsley suggested hopefully to his sister.

Wednesday shook her head. "There's no point. Someone would rescue Pubert before anything *good* happened. But I have another idea. We'll guillotine him!"

Setting up a guillotine was easy. They'd done it lots of times. But seconds before their guillotine sliced off his head, Pubert flung up a tiny hand and stopped the blade.

Wednesday scowled. She'd have to come up with something else. . . .

An owl hooted in the dead elm tree behind the Addams mansion. Far off, another owl gave a dismal reply.

It was hours after nightfall, but Wednesday and Pugsley were just getting started. They were standing on the edge of the roof and staring down into the misty dark.

It was time for a little physics project.

In Wednesday's arms was her baby brother. She had "borrowed" him from his cradle to help with the experiment.

In Pugsley's arms was a cannonball.

"The baby weighs ten pounds," Wednesday announced. "The cannonball weighs twenty pounds. Which one will hit the stone walkway first?"

Pugsley knitted his brow. "I'm still on fractions in school," he said after a second.

"Well, which do you *think?*" asked Wednesday.

"Uh . . . the cannonball?"

Wednesday nodded approvingly. "Very good. But which one will bounce?"

"Uh . . . the baby?"

Wednesday shrugged. "There's only one way to find out," she said. "Ready? One . . . two . . . three. . . ."

Pubert and the cannonball plummeted down into the dark.

At that exact instant, Gomez leaned out of his bedroom window to check for rain. A few raindrops landed on his outstretched hands. Then his new son landed *in* his outstretched hands.

Gomez and Morticia stared at each other in dismay. "Oh, dear," said Morticia faintly.

This was really getting to be quite a problem. They needed help.

And that was how Morticia and Pubert came to join a New Moms' Support Group.

Dr. Whalen-Shaffler was a very, very concerned therapist. She cared about her clients in a very, very concerned way. As she gazed around her office at the latest New Moms' Support Group, her only thought was how she could prove her concern to them.

"Let's begin by just going around the room and introducing ourselves," she suggested with a super-sincere smile.

The first mother spoke up eagerly. "I'm Judy Morgan, and this is Rebecca Marjorie," she said, holding her adorable pink-cheeked baby up for inspection. (Morticia winced and turned away.) "She's a *joy*. She's just *perfect*. But my husband says I get too worried about her. Do any of you have this problem?"

Morticia spoke right up. "I know just how you feel. Last week, my baby was missing for three days. For the first two days I was fine—but by Friday, I was, frankly, upset. I looked everywhere. The swamp, the crypt, the trunk of the car. And do you know where he was? The attic!" she finished triumphantly. "Locked in a steamer trunk safe and sound! So don't worry. Babies are like mildew. They always come back.

"*My* problem is with my two other children," Morticia went on as the other mothers stared at her openmouthed. "They're very jealous of the new baby. Once they tied him to the lightning rod. Once they left him on the road, covered with leaves. And just this morning, there he was in the garage—covered with honey and red ants." She shook her head ruefully. "Kids!"

Dr. Whalen-Shaffler was horrified—and very, very concerned. Unfortunately, she couldn't think of anything to suggest. And for some reason, none of the other mothers in the group seemed to feel very comfortable around Morticia.

So Morticia and Gomez decided to forget about Dr. Whalen-Shaffler and hold an Addams family meeting instead. They summoned the children, Granny, and Lurch to the Great Room and asked them to sit down.

"Children, why do you hate the baby?" Gomez asked them kindly.

Pugsley shrugged. "We don't *hate* him," he answered uncomfortably. "We just want to play with him."

"Especially his head," Wednesday added.

"Do you think we love the baby more than we love you?" Gomez went on.

Both Wednesday and Pugsley nodded.

Now Morticia chimed in. "Do you think that when a new baby arrives, one of the other children has to die?"

"Yes," Wednesday and Pugsley answered in unison.

Granny leaned forward and patted them on the cheeks. "That's just not true," she said soothingly. "Not nowadays!"

"Of course it isn't true," said Morticia. "All mothers have favorites, naturally. Just as all mothers have children whom they hate. But they wouldn't *kill* those children. Usually just walling them up is enough."

She spoke convincingly, but the children didn't believe her. Which is probably why Gomez found the baby in the snakepit a few hours later.

The baby was fine, but Gomez had had enough. He decided to hire a nanny for Pubert.

A nanny who could double as a bodyguard.

CHAPTER THREE

DEBBIE GOES TO WORK

*T*o say the least, Debbie Jellinsky looked out of place in the Addams mansion. She had curly blond hair, a spotless white nanny's uniform, and a beaming smile. The beaming smile didn't waver even when she saw Lurch for the first time.

"Addams residence?" she asked perkily as Lurch swung open the huge front door. Then, when she saw Morticia behind Lurch—"Hi! Hi! I'm Debbie Jellinsky. The nannies' agency sent me. Are you the mom?"

Morticia paused. She had never in her life been referred to as a "mom."

"I am Mrs. Addams," she said in a frosty voice.

"I love your dress," Debbie chirped, unfazed. "It's so tight!"

Gomez was just coming down the stairs, and Morticia turned to him. "Gomez," she said uncertainly, "I believe we may have a new nanny. Miss Jellinsky."

"Debbie," Debbie corrected her. She now aimed her radiant smile at Gomez. "Aren't you the lady-killer!" she gushed.

"I was acquitted," Gomez said cheerfully.

Morticia brought the conversation back to business. "Now, before you meet the baby," she said briskly, "have you had your shots? Mumps? Measles? Rabies?"

Debbie nodded. "Sure have! I can't wait to see your little fella. I just love babies. They're so sweet and pink and innocent, I just want to grab them and squeeze them until there's not a breath left in their tiny little bodies!"

Morticia and Gomez exchanged a look. At last they'd found the help they were looking for!

While this conversation was taking place downstairs, three other Addamses were silently watching from upstairs. Two of the three were Wednesday and Pugsley, who were spying on Debbie through the bannister.

The third was Uncle Fester, who was spying on Debbie *over* the bannister. But unlike Wednesday and Pugsley, who were frowning suspiciously at the new nanny, Fester was smiling so hard that he was almost drooling. His cavernous eyes flashed in their dark sockets, and his fish-white skin was flushed a dark red.

Uncle Fester had fallen head over heels in love.

"Ooooooh! I think there's one *big* fella I haven't met yet," said Debbie coyly. Uncle Fester ducked out of sight behind a column. "Hi there, Mister," called Debbie.

"Fester, come down," said Morticia. To Debbie, she added, "He's shy with living people. Fester, this is Miss Jellinsky, our new nanny."

Fester hadn't had much experience with girls. At the sight of Debbie, he was speechless. A little steam puffed out of his ears, but that was all. His silence didn't seem to faze Debbie, however.

"Hello, Fester," Debbie crowed, batting her long, thick, fake eyelashes. She shook her head in wonder and turned back to Morticia. "Where do you *find* these Addams men? I can't wait to start working here! I'll start first thing tomorrow!"

Debbie's first day as a nanny started easily enough. She waved good-bye to Morticia, Gomez, and Fester as they left to do some errands. Then she pulled Pubert to safety just before Wednesday and Pugsley dropped an anvil on him—and she didn't turn a hair.

"Look at you," she said soothingly to the two older children. "All cooped up in the house with a new baby. That's not easy, is it?"

"No," Pugsley blurted out.

"Why, I bet sometimes you wish it was still just the two of you!" Debbie went on.

"Or less," said Wednesday curtly.

Debbie flashed her megasmile. "Well, don't you two worry. Everything's going to be just fine."

She blew them a kiss and carried Pubert down the hall as Wednesday and Pugsley stared at her in disgust.

"We're going to do a little exploring, brat," Debbie muttered into the baby's hairy ear.

Down the long, dark hall she tiptoed, past cases filled with long-dead stuffed animals, until she reached the room she was looking for: Gomez's office. Debbie rummaged around in a closet until she found a ball and chain to anchor the baby. Then she got to work.

It only took her five minutes to find Uncle Fester's financial ledgers. Debbie scanned them rapidly, pulling out document after document.

"My, my," she murmured under her breath. "Fester Addams is a wealthy man. Stocks and bonds . . . deeds . . ." She gasped. *"Gold!"*

She stared up at the ceiling, thinking hard—so hard that she didn't notice Wednesday staring at her from her hiding place across the room. Of course it would have been hard for anyone to notice Wednesday. She had painted herself to match the wallpaper.

"What a strange old house," Debbie mused aloud. "So drafty. It's really no place for children." There was a hint of menace in her voice now.

"No place at all."

* * *

"Stop it, Pubert!" Debbie snapped a few hours later. She was reaching into the cradle, trying to get the baby dressed. "Hold still, you little brat!"

"He's not a brat," came Wednesday's clear voice from the doorway.

Startled, Debbie turned around. "Of—of course he's not," she said, trying to get her smile organized. "He's an adorable little baby. We're getting him all ready for a nice walk. Would you like to come?"

"Are you a real nanny?" was Wednesday's reply.

Debbie's jaw dropped. "Why, what a question!" she said with a flustered laugh. She shook her curls fetchingly. "Of course I am!"

Wednesday continued to stare at her. "Why did you come here?" she asked.

"To—to take care of you. All of you!"

Now Wednesday's eyes were burning with anger. "Especially my uncle?" she asked.

Debbie did her best to laugh it off, but she was more worried than she showed.

The kid's on to me, she thought. She's not as dumb as most children. I'm going to have to think of something fast.

Unfortunately for Wednesday, Debbie was a very fast thinker.

"I can't believe it," moaned Morticia brokenly that evening. "What have we done wrong?"

Morticia and Gomez were sitting on a loveseat in the Great Room and staring at Debbie in horror. She was in a chair facing them, cuddling Pubert and fixing the Addamses with an earnest gaze.

"I shouldn't be telling you this," she said in a confidential voice. "Wednesday and Pugsley swore me to secrecy, the little angels. But it's all they want. It's all they talked about all morning. They're just afraid to ask you. You see, they're afraid you'll think that— that they don't love you."

Morticia let her hands fall open in her lap. "The poor things. Of course we love them. It's just such a . . . bizarre request!"

"It's terrifying," said Gomez with a shudder.

Debbie leaned forward. "They have their hearts set on it," she assured the worried parents. "I knew you'd want to know. As concerned, caring parents and all."

Morticia looked helplessly at her husband. "Oh, Gomez, what do you think?"

He stared back at her in equal confusion. "How can we say no?" he asked.

Debbie leaned back in her chair with a triumphant gleam in her eye. "Now, don't even mention this to the children," she said quickly. "Just do it. I'm sure they'll deny everything, God love 'em. But they really want to go.

"They really *want* to go to sleep-away camp for the whole entire summer."

It was a week later.

Wednesday and Pugsley had planned the perfect escape. They had waited until everyone was asleep. They had slid down the exit chutes outside their bedroom windows with their luggage in hand. They had picked up their suitcases and begun to steal away into the night. They had done everything right—except for realizing that Uncle Fester would be staying up late to give a vine in the garden a blood transfusion.

"Children?" he called.

Wednesday and Pugsley dropped their luggage in despair and turned to face him.

"Where are you going?" Uncle Fester asked.

"We're running away," Wednesday said grimly. "Mother and Father want to kill us. They want to drop us into a pot of boiling oil. They want us to live in misery."

"You mean . . . summer camp?" asked Uncle Fester, mystified.

Wednesday nodded. "Why did they listen to that woman?" she wailed.

"That woman?" asked Uncle Fester alertly. "Was it—um—Debbie's idea?"

"That's what *I* think," said Wednesday, and Pugsley nodded. "Mother and Father never mentioned camp until that schemer came here to take care of moldy little Pubert."

Uncle Fester cleared his throat. "Well, if it was her idea, maybe it's for the best," he said rapidly. "Debbie's very wise. And very caring."

Wednesday gave him a look. "And very blond."

"Do you *like* her, Uncle Fester?" Pugsley asked in amazement.

Fester dropped everything he was holding and

19

started to gibber. "No. No, I don't. Well. No! Well, she's very nice. For a nanny! She's . . . she's tops!"

"Uncle Fester!" Wednesday scolded him. "Get a grip!"

But both of the children had a terrible feeling it was too late for that.

And too late for them.

CHAPTER FOUR

ALOHA, CAMP CHIPPEWA

*T*he Addams family's huge black town car didn't drive very fast. It was too old for that. Mostly, it lumbered along, wheezing.

But on the day the car set out for summer camp, it seemed to race. As Lurch pulled in through the gates of the camp, Wednesday and Pugsley both felt they'd never taken such a brief, awful trip.

"Camp Chippewa," Morticia read aloud as they drove through the gate and passed a sign printed (in twig-and-pine-cone letters) with the camp's name. "How . . . charming," she added, trying to be upbeat.

"What's a Chippewa?" asked Pugsley.

"It's an old Indian word," his father told him.

"It means 'orphan,'" Wednesday added bleakly.

Cars and vans were streaming through the gate as

other families arrived to drop off their children. Counselors were hugging returning favorites. Kids were dashing everywhere, laughing and calling to one another. The sun was shining, and on the horizon the lake was glinting blue. To the Addamses, it was a vision of pure horror.

As the car pulled into a parking space, Wednesday realized that she was being watched. Standing outside the car was a girl about twelve years old. A very pretty girl, wearing very expensive braces, very expensive camping gear, and a very self-satisfied expression. Wednesday shuddered as she opened the door. What creepy planet is she from? she wondered to herself, unaware that the other girl was asking herself the identical question.

Gomez stepped from the car and took a deep breath. "Fresh air!" he exclaimed heartily. "The scent of pine!"

Silently Lurch handed him a cigar to take away the stench.

"Wednesday, look at all the other children," Morticia coaxed. "Their freckles. Their bright little eyes. Their eager, friendly expressions. Help them," she begged her daughter.

The expensive twelve-year-old was still staring at the Addamses. "Hi, I'm Amanda Buckman," she proclaimed. "Why are you dressed like that?" She peered at Wednesday as though she were staring at a wasp under a magnifying glass.

"Like what?" asked Wednesday blankly.

"Like you're going to a funeral! Why are you dressed as though someone died?"

"Just wait." Wednesday's voice was dark. "Someone will."

Amanda's father was making his own attempts to break the ice. "Hi there. Don Buckman," he said to Gomez, shaking hands with vigor. "Isn't this place something else? Very exclusive, you know."

"Really," Gomez said doubtfully. He stepped aside with a grimace as a Frisbee flew over his head. "How so?"

"A kid has to be extra-special to get in here," Don boasted. "Gifted. Exceptional. Our Amanda has already skipped two grades. How about your boy?"

"He's on probation," Gomez told him, putting a proud arm around Pugsley's shoulder.

"We just *love* Chippewa," Amanda's mother was babbling to Morticia. "Amanda couldn't *wait* to get here. It's *all* she talked about. She's got a whole new wardrobe." She glanced at Wednesday. "And *this* little lady?"

Morticia gave her a confiding smile. "Wednesday's at that very special age. You know—when a girl has only one thing on her mind."

Ellen pinched Wednesday's cheek. *"Boys?"* she squealed.

"Homicide," Wednesday growled through clenched teeth.

The shrill blast of a whistle drowned out Mrs. Buckman's reply. Everyone turned to see a youngish man and his youngish wife standing on a little platform near the flagpole.

Wednesday's heart sank even farther down in her chest. They look like mutant Boy Scouts, she thought to herself.

It was true. Gary and Becky Granger, Camp Chippewa's directors, were the preppiest, peppiest couple in the world, and perhaps in the universe. Both of them had wide, gleaming smiles and narrow, camp-obsessed minds. Morticia glanced at their khaki shorts and sensible footwear and gave a little shiver of distaste.

"Listen up, everyone!" Gary called, clapping his hands. (He had a super-loud clap, Wednesday noticed.) "I'm Gary Granger!"

"And I'm Becky Morton Granger!" his wife yelled, clapping a few times herself.

"We're the owners and directors here at Camp Chippewa, America's foremost facility for privileged young adults!" Gary shouted.

"And we're all here to learn, to grow, and to just plain have fun!" Becky shrieked.

"'Cause that's what being privileged is all ABOUT!" Gary finished in a bellow.

Mr. Buckman patted Amanda on the shoulder. "That's right, hon," he whispered. "Impressive thinking."

Suddenly there was a wheezing sound behind him. The Buckmans and the Addamses turned to see one last camper and his family straggling up to the assembled crowd.

This camper looked even less happy to be at Camp Chippewa than Wednesday and Pugsley. He was a spindly, pale boy with glasses and knock knees. He was clutching an inhaler tightly in one hand.

The boy's mother swatted him across the shoulders. "Stand up straight, Joel!" she hissed in a whisper.

Joel coughed.

"Smile!" Mr. Glicker ordered him.

"I can't breathe," Joel said hoarsely. He took a frantic pull on his inhaler. Amanda's father rolled his eyes in disgust.

"Wednesday, Pugsley—it's time for us to leave," Morticia said gently. "Lurch is waiting. And Father and I want to get home before the baby eats something he shouldn't. Like Debbie's foot. Write us when you get a chance, darlings."

"Oh, we'll write you, all right," muttered Wednesday as she watched her parents climbing into the town car. "You'll have our suicide notes by dawn tomorrow."

Unfortunately, it turned out that Camp Chippewa's busy schedule didn't allow much time for committing suicide. Wednesday and Pugsley were both still alive when the first swim session started that afternoon.

The two of them stood on the dock with Amanda Buckman and a group of other campers as Gary Granger blew his whistle a few hundred times.

"LIFESAVING!" he suddenly yelled. (Wednesday and Pugsley flinched at the sound.) "I know we're all top-notch l'il swimmers, and now we get to show our

25

stuff! Let's have our first pair of lifesaving buddies. Amanda and Wednesday!"

Amanda stared at Wednesday and curled her lip. "Is that your *bathing suit?*" she drawled, pointing at Wednesday's full-length, all-black suit.

Wednesday smiled sweetly. "Is that your overbite?" she asked, pointing at Amanda's mouth.

Amanda flushed angrily, but Gary Granger was speaking again. "Now," he said, "one of you will be the drowning victim, and one of you will be our lifesaver."

"I'll be the victim!" Amanda said eagerly. "I'm going to be an actress when I grow up!"

"Great!" said Gary. "Now, Amanda, you jump in, swim out a few yards, and start drowning. Then Wednesday can rescue you."

Amanda leaped gracefully into the lake and flung her arms over her head.

"Help me! Please, won't someone help me!" she called in a musical voice, splashing a few decorative drops of water into the air. "Help me! I'm dying!"

Wednesday turned to Gary. "I can't swim," she told him proudly.

The crickets and tree frogs were beginning to chirp. The birds were sleepily ending their songs. Bats were starting to swoop through the air. As Pugsley watched them, he felt a little better. *At least they have bats here,* he thought.

Even the longest first days of camp must eventually

come to an end, and so it was for Wednesday and Pugsley. They pretended to eat their Sloppy Joes, pretended to sing "Michael, Row the Boat Ashore," and pretended to brush their teeth. (Morticia never made them brush their teeth. "Minty freshness is vulgar," she had said when they were packing their foot lockers for camp. "But you have to get to know all sorts of people in this world. You'd better take toothbrushes with you just in case.") Then they climbed into their bunks and lay there, rigid with misery. The air was too fresh, and the night was too peaceful. How could a person get any sleep here?

At least the girls in Wednesday's cabin weren't trying to sleep. They had decided to tell ghost stories instead.

All the girls were lying on their bunks in their pajamas. They were aiming their flashlights at Amanda Buckman, who was in the middle of a story she swore had happened to the friend of a friend.

". . . And then the ghost said, 'IIII WIIILLLL HAAUUNT YOOOUUU FOREEEEVER!' " Amanda wailed.

"Eeeeeeeeeeeeeee," said the girls halfheartedly.

"Now it's your turn, Wednesday. You have to continue the ghost story," Amanda ordered.

Wednesday sighed. "I don't want to. This is dumb."

Amanda's lips tightened. "If you can't do it—" she began.

Wednesday sighed even more gustily and raised herself up on her elbows. "All right. All right. So—uh

—so the next night, the ghost came back to the haunted cabin. And he said to the campers, 'None of you really believes in me. So I will have to prove my powers.' And the next morning, when the campers woke up . . . all of their nose jobs were gone and all their old noses had grown back."

The cabin erupted in earsplitting shrieks of terror.

CHAPTER FIVE

FOR
THE LOVE
OF FESTER

*B*ack at the Addams mansion, Pubert was also being told a story. But even if he had been old enough to understand it, he wouldn't have listened to it. He was sound asleep in his cobwebby cradle.

Debbie, his nanny, didn't care about that. She knew that her real audience was outside the door, not inside the cradle. Uncle Fester was standing out in the hall, listening spellbound to the tale Debbie was telling.

". . . And everyone at the ball turned and stared at Cinderella," Debbie said gently. " 'Who is that beautiful woman?' everyone asked."

Fester inched a little closer to the door.

"Even Prince Charming noticed the new arrival," Debbie went on. " 'Who are you?' he asked Cinderella."

The door creaked the tiniest bit. Debbie raised her voice ever so slightly.

"'My name is Cinderella,' she said to the prince. 'And could you tell me—who is that man over by the punch bowl? That fascinating man? That oddly sensual man? That man who makes me quiver inside? That *bald* man?'"

Fester's eyes were wide with wonder. It's not possible, he thought. She could never love someone like me.

And, of course, he was right.

That was only the beginning of Debbie's campaign. The next morning, when Gomez and Morticia had returned from Camp Chippewa, Debbie drifted into the conservatory. Morticia was there already, painting a picture of Thing. (Thing liked posing for portraits, especially when it got to wear jewelry.)

"Mrs. Addams?" Debbie's voice was shy. "Could I ask you something of a . . . personal nature?"

"Of course," said Morticia warmly.

Debbie did her best to blush. "It's just—well, you seem so worldly. So sophisticated. I can see that you know everything about—love."

"Merci," Morticia murmured absently, without taking her eyes off her work.

"Well, I was just wondering. Is Fester—is Fester seeing anyone?"

Morticia shook her head. "You mean, is there a woman in Fester's life? Or in his luggage? No, Debbie—sadly, no.

"I've always wondered about that," Morticia continued. "Fester Addams . . . he's bloated. He's pasty. He *reeks.*" She smiled teasingly. "If I weren't already married . . ."

"Oh, I know!" Debbie agreed quickly. "I feel just the same, except that I've never been married." Then she bit her lip and looked down again. "I'm sorry, Mrs. Addams. Please go on with your work. I didn't mean to interrupt."

"It's all right," Morticia told her. "My hand has fallen asleep."

She pointed to the pedestal. Thing had just toppled over, exhausted.

While this woman-to-woman chat was going on, Fester and Gomez were in Gomez's study having a little talk of their own. (Gomez, who liked efficiency, was signing documents with one hand and playing a game of darts with the other. This game was upsetting to Lurch, who was holding the dartboard in front of his chest. He didn't like to see Gomez get distracted with a dart in his hand.)

"Debbie. *Debbie,*" Fester moaned, writhing in his chair. "Even the sound of her name! *Debbie.* Isn't it beautiful? It makes me think of . . . vinyl. Chemicals. Poison!"

Gomez stared at his brother with deep emotion, and threw a dart without looking. Hastily Lurch lurched—and caught the dart on the dartboard.

"Bull's-eye! Fester!" Gomez exclaimed. "Truly? Has it finally happened? At long last?"

"I don't know!" Fester said frantically. "I think so!"

He clasped his hands together.

"All these years, Gomez, I've watched you and Morticia. From windows. Doorways. Keyholes. I've been so happy for you, but I have to confess, I've been jealous, too. Why, there were times when—when I wanted to see both of you decapitated, hanging on meat hooks!" He passed a hand over his sweating head.

Gomez nodded sympathetically. "Morticia and I have also talked about that," he said, throwing another dart. (Lurch caught that one, too.)

"And now," Fester went on, "now, maybe . . . dare I? Dare I ask Debbie to . . . dinner? What if she says no? What if she says *yes?* Oh, Gomez! If I ask her, will you come? You and Morticia?"

"Of course we will," said his brother simply. He threw another dart. Lurch caught that one, too.

In his mouth.

That night, when the moon was full and the moths were swarming, Gomez and Morticia met at the family cemetery to talk things over. They were both in foul moods. The day's news had unsettled them badly.

"Fester," Morticia said dully.

"Debbie," Gomez replied in a listless monotone.

Morticia bit her lip. "She's blond. Blue-eyed."

"Good with children." Sadly Gomez shook his head.

"A—a lovely young woman." Morticia could hardly choke the words out.

Gomez put a hand on his wife's shoulder. "I know, my darling. I know. It's not pleasant. But he loves her."

"Yes, but—I'd hoped for so much more for Fester!" Morticia cried. "Someone with breeding! Elegance! Scars!"

"It's true," Gomez agreed. "Our dear mother, on her deathbed, had only one request. 'Find Fester a wife,' she said. 'Search far and wide. Drain the swamps. . . .'"

There was a long, melancholy silence. Finally Morticia broke it. "Still, Debbie seems devoted to Fester," she pointed out. "And she *is* very sweet. I'll do what I can to change that, of course. Something with her hair first, I think."

Her husband nodded with sudden determination. "And for Fester, I'll—Morticia, I'll do it! *I'll give him a bath!*"

At bathtime, Fester's screams terrified the country-side for miles around.

Le Vaisseau Sanguin—The Blood Vessel—was the Addams family's favorite bistro. It wasn't often that they came across a place that offered such a decaying atmosphere *and* such putrid food. The peeling, blood-colored paint, the gloomy lights, the smell of rot that wafted through the air every time one of the waiters opened the kitchen door—what better spot for romance?

Morticia and Gomez thought so, anyway. So did

Fester, although he was too nervous to speak. And as for Debbie—well, perhaps it was lucky no one knew what Debbie was thinking.

"This is just lovely," she said perkily, glancing around. "Isn't it, Fester?

"Fester?" she repeated.

"Fester?"

Fester just sat there, goggling at her. A half-chewed roll stuck out of his mouth like a crazy tongue.

"Fester!" Gomez said sharply.

With a start, Fester grabbed the soggy roll from his mouth and held it out to Debbie.

"Oh!" Debbie gasped. "Oh, I—"

"It's a quaint French custom, sharing half-eaten bread," Morticia broke in quickly.

"Fester is truly continental," Gomez added, trying to cover for his brother. "He's spent many years abroad. He speaks twelve languages fluently."

Debbie's face brightened. "I could tell!" she said. "You know, when I first saw him, I *thought* he was from Europe! He has that . . . certain charm."

Fester's face puckered up with confusion. "I do?" he said plaintively. "But I never wear that charm in front of people! I keep it hidden in the mausoleum!"

Morticia jumped to her feet. "Speaking of charms, how about a trip to the powder room?" she asked Debbie. "Gomez and Fester can catch up on current events while we're gone." She shot her husband a meaningful look. *Pull Fester together!* it said.

In the ladies' room, Morticia reapplied her blood-red lipstick. "Fester is really a wonderful man," she said coaxingly. "He's just terribly shy."

"Really?" Debbie sounded doubtful. "Are you sure? I just can't tell! Does he like me at *all?*"

"Of course he does!" Morticia assured her. "He vomited," she pointed out.

Debbie grimaced down at the stain on the front of her dress. "That's true," she said ruefully. "Does he always do—uh—*this* with women he likes?"

"Oh, no," Morticia promised. "Just you."

Well, that's a plus, Debbie told herself sarcastically.

Back at the table, Gomez was trying to give Fester some brotherly advice. It wasn't going down too well. Fester was too worried about having thrown up all over his date.

"Do you think Debbie minded?" he asked Gomez.

"Of course not," Gomez said heartily. "She *adores* you, Fester!"

Fester was gnawing his own fingers in frustration. "Oh, I'm making such a mess of this!" he wailed. "Gomez, how do you do it? How can I be like you? How can I be . . . suave?"

His older brother leaned forward. "Woo her, Fester," he said throatily. "Admire her. Make her feel as though she's the most sublime creature on earth— Ah, here come the ladies. Fester, this is your chance!"

"We're back," Morticia announced. "Noses powdered."

Gomez bowed his head in a courtly manner. Fester watched him intently, trying to pick up a cue.

"Perfection achieved," Gomez told the two women. His voice was as lush as a river of melted chocolate. "We are the luckiest brothers on earth. We are unworthy of such splendor . . . undeserving of such radiance."

He turned to Fester and raised a silken eyebrow.

"That's right," Fester blurted out. "We're unworthy, for sure. We should have brought—uh—*ugly* girls!"

Gomez swallowed a sigh. Fester had a lot to learn about technique.

Now, for example, he was tenderly caressing Debbie's hand—with his fork.

"How you must hate me," Debbie said bitterly a few hours later. She and Fester were taking a midnight stroll through the cemetery.

"What? Hate you?" Fester repeated.

Debbie's chin was trembling. "Here you are, a debonair man of the world. How I must bore you!"

"Never!" Fester's voice was full of passion.

"With your . . . looks . . . and your charm, women must follow you everywhere," Debbie continued. She cast a sly glance upward to see how Fester was taking this.

"Just store detectives," Fester said dolefully.

This is my chance! Debbie stopped in the path, turned to face Fester, and took his clammy hand in hers. Her voice throbbed out into the night like a big fake bell.

"Until now, I thought it was impossible," she said boldly. "And I shouldn't be saying this. But Fester Addams, *I love you!*"

Fester looked as though she'd trained a police hose on him. "You do?" he asked.

"I do." Debbie gave a dramatic sigh. "Please be brutally honest with me, Fester. I have to know. How do you feel about"—Debbie turned her face shyly away—"about me?"

"I love you!" Fester bellowed. "I worship you! I'd do anything for you! *Anything!*"

"Oh, *Fester!*" Debbie's voice broke with just the right tinge of emotion. "First of all, buy some deodorant!"

Overcome with passion, Fester swept her into his arms, and they shared their first kiss.

Neither of the lovers noticed the black widow spider scuttling across the monument that towered above them. For a second the spider paused above Debbie's head, as if in warning. Then it darted out of sight.

Back in the house, Morticia and Gomez were also sharing a quiet moment together in Pubert's room. "This evening," Gomez told his wife, "as I watched Fester and Debbie, I kept my fingers crossed. I hoped."

"I prayed," Morticia said tenderly.

"'Let them fall in love,' I said."

"Let them know happiness," Morticia added. "Let them—"

At that moment Fester came thudding into the room. "Gomez! Morticia!" He panted. "Great news! Something impossible! A miracle!"

"Your rash is gone?" Gomez asked in amazement.

"No! No! I'm engaged!"

Fester beckoned toward the door, and in a moment Debbie slipped shyly in. She looked radiant, but maybe that was just the light glinting off her massive diamond ring.

"That ring . . ." Morticia breathed.

For the merest fraction of a second, a shadow crossed Gomez's face. "It was our mother's," he said curtly. "She was buried with it."

Triumphantly Debbie brandished a dirt-encrusted shovel in his face. And then she and Fester melted once again into a passionate kiss.

Through the barred window, a massive bolt of lightning shot menacingly through the sky.

Now it was still later—so late that even Morticia and Gomez had gone to their chamber. In fact, only one pair of eyes was open in the Addams house. They belonged to Debbie Jellinsky, Fester's new fiancée.

She was lying in bed watching "America's Most Disgusting Unsolved Crimes" on her little black-and-white TV. It wasn't her favorite show, but she had a particular interest in seeing it tonight.

"Tonight," the host announced, "we will investigate the case of Ursula, Carmen, and Nadine."

Three pictures flashed onto the screen. First came

Ursula, who looked exactly like Debbie disguised as a Scandinavian blond. Second came Carmen, who, strangely enough, looked exactly like Debbie disguised as a dark-haired Latin woman. Third came Nadine, a redheaded bombshell, who just happened to look exactly like Debbie in a red wig.

The real Debbie's lips tightened in fury as she watched the screen. At that moment, Fester wouldn't have recognized her at all.

"Three very different women, with one thing in common," said the show's host. *"Murder."*

Thunder rumbled ominously overhead. In his own bedroom, Fester turned over uneasily in his sleep.

"They are all the same woman," continued the host. "She is known by the police as the Black Widow. Like the Black Widow spider, she marries—and then she kills. She hunts down wealthy men, finding the richest bachelors. She marries them. And on the wedding night she kills them."

The host lowered his voice. "The deaths look accidental," he said solemnly. "And after the funeral, the Black Widow disappears, cash in hand. But the money never lasts. And soon the Black Widow is hungry again. Hungry for cash—and hungry for love."

Debbie frowned to herself. "You moron," she whispered at the screen. "I'm not hungry for *love.*"

"The Black Widow is a mistress of disguise," said the host. "She has eluded the authorities for years. Who is she? And where will she turn up next?"

He smiled grimly. "All we can say is: Bachelors, beware!"

Far, far away, at Camp Chippewa, a jagged bolt of lightning suddenly tore through the sky. Wednesday's eyes flew open, and she sat upright in her bunk.

She didn't know what had awakened her. But she knew something was terribly wrong.

Back at home, someone needed her help.

CHAPTER SIX

THE HARMONY HUT

*O*ur Fester," crowed Granny Addams the next morning. "Engaged to be married!" She beamed down at Fester, who was holding hands with Debbie at the breakfast table. Both were wearing gleaming smiles, or at least Debbie was. Fester's teeth were too rotten to gleam.

"Would you like some porridge, Fester, dear?" Granny asked, taking down a saucepan.

"Yes, please!" said Fester brightly. "Today I'm so happy, I could eat a horse!"

"Suit yourself," said Granny. "Let me just get a different pot."

"We're all so excited for the two of you," said Morticia politely. I'll be a good sport about this if it kills me, she thought. And it probably will. "Debbie, we'd love to meet your family. And have them for dinner," she went on.

Granny ran a pointed tongue over her lips. "Are they big people?" she asked Debbie. "Meaty?"

But instead of answering, Debbie burst into tears. She buried her blond head in Fester's shoulder and shook with loud, fake sobs.

"Angel, what's the matter?" asked Fester, worried. "Can I get you anything? A hankie? A straitjacket?"

"No, no." Debbie gave a dainty sniff and wiped her eyes. "Y-you're all so kind," she quavered. "It's just that . . . it's just that . . ." She sniffed again. "You see, there was a horrible accident years ago, when I was just a child. An explosion. My entire family—" Her voice broke, and she couldn't go on.

"An explosion?" echoed Fester.

"Nothing left?" asked Gomez.

"Arms?" suggested Granny eagerly.

Debbie shook her head. "Nothing. No one."

"Well," said Morticia with sudden decision, "from now on *we* are your family. Everything we own is yours." She pushed aside her plateful of scrambled fungus and reached over to pat Debbie's arm.

Debbie glanced up alertly from her tissue. "Do you have a complete list of everything you own?" she asked in a businesslike voice.

Gomez didn't hear the question. "And as for the wedding," he announced, "it will be our pleasure. Every detail. We insist!"

Another fake tear trickled down Debbie's cheek. But this time, it was a fake tear of happiness.

42

"You people," she said, shaking her head in wonder. "There's just so much love in this room!"

"Mail call! Mail call!"

Miles and miles away from the Addams's love-filled kitchen, Wednesday was reading a letter from home. So were all the campers in Camp Chippewa's rec room. But Wednesday was the only one who looked as if her letter smelled like rotten eggs.

"Oh, no," she murmured as she read it. *"No."*

"What is it?" Pugsley asked.

Wednesday's voice rose an octave. "This is *unspeakable.*"

"Is something wrong, Wednesday?" asked Becky Granger, the camp's co-director. She and Gary were passing out the mail in the middle of the rec room.

"Wrong!" Wednesday burst out. "This is the worst thing that has ever happened in the history of human events!" She turned to Pugsley and wailed, "Uncle Fester is getting *married!"*

"A wedding?" Gary chuckled. "But that's great news!"

"To whom is he getting married?" asked Amanda Buckman prissily. Amanda always wanted to know everything about everyone.

Wednesday's shoulders sagged. "To the nanny," she said in a small, defeated voice.

"Yuck! Get out of this *room!"* Now Amanda looked as if *she* smelled something bad. "I mean, I'd kill myself if that happened to my uncle. He's marrying the *help?"*

43

"Come on, Mandy," put in Becky. "I'm sure she's a very nice lady."

"Yeah, right." Amanda snorted. "I think it's disgusting. I think their whole family is like some weird medical experiment." She tossed her head haughtily. "I think they're like circus people."

"What did you say?" Pugsley hissed.

"Campers!" Becky clapped her hands sharply. "Time for a group hug! Right away!"

The Chippewa campers were well trained. Quickly they all drew together into a big, warm huddle. All except Wednesday and Pugsley, that is. They hovered on the fringes of the group, staring at the other kids in disgust.

Gary shook a teasing finger at them. "Wednesday! Pugsley! Will a hug hurt us?"

"We don't hug," said Wednesday with dignity.

Becky moved lovingly toward the two children, arms outstretched. "I bet they're just shy," she said to her husband over her shoulder.

Both children took a giant step backward to get out of her way. "We're *not* shy," Pugsley protested. "We're contagious!"

But now Gary was frowning. He folded his arms and stared at Wednesday and Pugsley in silence for a few seconds. Gradually the rec room fell silent, too. No one wanted to miss seeing what happened to nonhuggers at Camp Chippewa.

Gary cleared his throat. "Y'know, I'm sensing some real friction here," he said slowly. "Something not quite . . . *Chippewa*. But *hey!"* He clapped his hands so loudly that half the campers in the room covered their ears. "No problem-o! They'll come around! All they need are good friends, good fun, and"—his voice suddenly grew threatening again—"a little time in the Harmony Hut."

"The Harmony Hut? What's that?" Pugsley asked nervously.

Becky smiled, and for the first time the children noticed what big, gleaming teeth she had. "It's a very special place," she said. "A place where we go when we need to think about who we are—and who we should be."

The Harmony Hut was filled with light, scented with fresh flowers, and gently tinkling with wind chimes. It was gaily decorated in pastel colors and bright posters and lacy pillows and unicorns and trolls and pictures of the sunset and dolls and chintz and flouncy ruffled curtains.

It was the ugliest room Wednesday and Pugsley had ever seen—and now they were its prisoners. Half an hour ago Gary had dragged them in here. He hadn't said when he would be back to get them.

"How long do we have to stay here?" asked Pugsley, appalled.

"Until we crack," his sister replied grimly. "And the way things are going, that could be—" There was a scuffling sound at the Harmony Hut's front door. A small, thin boy clutching an asthma inhaler and a copy of *A Brief History of Time* suddenly appeared at the door of the hut. He tried to turn around, got a shove in the back, and stumbled forward into the room again. The door slammed behind him, and he collapsed into a flower-printed chair.

"Have fu-u-un!" the children heard Becky and Gary carol. Giggling together, the camp directors walked away.

The three children eyed one another warily.

"I saw you on the first day," Wednesday remembered. "What's your name?"

"Joel," the boy said, staring around the Harmony Hut with disgust.

"What're you in for?" asked Pugsley.

"I wouldn't go horseback riding."

"That's *all?*" Wednesday asked in disbelief.

Joel cleared his throat. "And I wouldn't make a birdhouse."

"Why not?"

Joel hung his head. "I—I just wanted to read."

As if he'd been lying in wait—which he probably had—Gary suddenly popped back into the room. He grabbed Joel's book and tucked it under his arm.

"No reading on *my* time, four-eyes," he said with a smirk. "See you later!"

The door slammed behind him. The children could hear him whistling "Zip-a-dee-doo-dah" as he headed down the path.

"I can't take this any longer," said Wednesday slowly. "I'm breaking out of this prison. The whole camp, I mean, not just the Harmony Hut. But maybe I can torch the Harmony Hut before I leave."

"I want to come with you," said Pugsley right away.

"And me?" Joel begged.

Wednesday nodded. "Sure. We can use our time in here to plan an escape. I want us out tonight, though," she said, thinking aloud. "I'm sure Chippewa causes cuteness. We've got to get out before we catch it."

Late at night Camp Chippewa was at its most beautiful. The lake waters gleamed softly, reflecting the stars. The cabins' tin roofs glowed gently, reflecting the moonlight. The barbed wire edging the camp boundary fences glinted harshly, reflecting the high-intensity searchlights installed at the guards' outposts to prevent escapees.

But Wednesday wasn't expecting any trouble. For one thing, all three children were wearing black, so it would be hard to spot them. For another, Pugsley and Wednesday were used to nighttime ventures. And it was turning out that Joel wasn't a bad accomplice to bring along, either. Like the Boy Scout he wasn't, Joel had come prepared.

He stared up at the barbed wire and reached for his backpack. Pulling out an enormous pair of wire cutters, he began to attack the barbed wire. "We don't want anyone getting tetanus," he said in a spitty whisper.

He carefully snipped the barbed-wire barricade open so that there was space to climb over the fence.

Then he motioned frantically at Wednesday. *"Go!"* he whispered.

Wednesday nodded and began to scramble up the fence. The boys were quick to follow her. In their black ninja suits, the children were practically invisible—

Unless you were a trained guard waiting at your outpost with a superstrong flashlight and a posse of attack dogs.

A siren began to blare. The dogs began to howl and tug at their chains. And Amanda Buckman, carrying a flashlight that would have blinded the sun itself, began to shriek at the top of her lungs.

"THERE THEY ARE! I SAW THEM SNEAKING OUT!"

Instantly Wednesday, Pugsley, and Joel were surrounded by everyone else in the whole camp. They stood there motionless, blinking in the bright lights and checking out the other campers' pajamas.

Gary stepped forward angrily. "Children!" he thundered. "What do you think you're *doing?"*

Wednesday fixed him with a cold, calm eye. "We have to see our family," she said icily. "It's important."

"More important than a summer of fun?" Becky snorted. (She was dressed in a plaid flannel nightgown layered over a polo shirt and hip waders.) "More important than making new friends? More important than *sharing?"*

"And Joel Glicker," Gary went on. "I'm surprised at you."

"I have to get out of here too," Joel stammered. "I, uh, I have allergies."

Becky shook her head incredulously. "You're allergic to sunshine? And arts? And *crafts?"* she shouted.

"Yup," was all Joel said.

Amanda Buckman, who had shoved her way to the front of the crowd, folded her arms and glared at the three escapees. "I think they should be punished," she said, tossing back her perfect hair.

The other campers loved the idea. "PU-NISH! PU-NISH! PU-NISH!" they started to chant, stamping their feet in rhythm. "PU-NISH! PU-NISH! PU—"

"No, no. We're not here to punish," Becky broke in reluctantly. "We're here to *inspire."*

"That's right," chimed in her husband. There was a savage light in his eye. "And campers, do you know what kind of inspiration our little ninja friends here need? Do you know what just might turn their sad and potentially wasted little lives right on around?"

Joel looked as though he were about to collapse with dread. "What?" he asked.

With a flourish, Becky pulled out her pitchpipe.

"No! No!" Joel yowled. "Not that! Not—"

But it was too late. The perfect children of Camp Chippewa were already forming a circle around the three little rebels.

Becky blew into the pitchpipe. "Hit it, gang," she said.

"KUM BA YAH, MY LORD," the Chippewa campers sang at the top of their lungs. "KUM BA

49

YAH. KUM BA YAH, MY LORD, KUM BA YAH . . ."

At the center of the circle, Wednesday, Pugsley, and Joel doubled up and fell writhing to their knees.

In all their lives they had never expected a revenge *this* deadly.

CHAPTER SEVEN

COUNTDOWN TO THE WEDDING!

If Gary and Becky Granger had hoped that "Kum Ba Yah" would drive the Addams children and Joel Glicker apart, they were disappointed. The ordeal only brought the friends closer together.

Joel loved hearing about life in the Addams family. Wednesday and Pugsley, for their part, were fascinated by how sickly Joel was. Especially Wednesday. She had never met anyone so likely to keel over on the spot.

"Are you *really* allergic?" she asked Joel suspiciously one afternoon when they were supposed to be playing volleyball.

"Uh-huh," Joel replied. "To almost everything." A volleyball hit him in the side of the head, but he ignored it.

"No, you're not," Wednesday scoffed.

"Am too!" Joel protested. "I can't have dairy products, or wear wool, or drink fluoridated water." Another volleyball hit him in the side of the head, but he ignored it. "And do you know what happens if my Mom uses fabric softener?"

"What?" .

"I die," said Joel proudly. Five volleyballs hit him in the side of the head, but he ignored them. So did Wednesday.

"Meet me in the infirmary at midnight," she whispered to Joel. "There's something else I want to talk about."

Joel nodded just before an entire volley of volleyballs hit him in the side of the head. "GLICKER!" yelled his angry teammates.

"Someone's not trying," said Becky threateningly.

Hastily Wednesday, Pugsley, and Joel tried to get into the spirit of things. Even volleyball couldn't be worse than another round of "Kum Ba Yah."

Camp Chippewa's infirmary wasn't used much. ("A sick person is a bad sport," Gary always said.) At midnight, the infirmary was used even less. In the moonlight, it looked like a medical classroom from an earlier time.

What do they need a skeleton for? Wednesday wondered to herself, staring at the full-size human skeleton hanging on a stand in one corner. Just making the place more homelike, I guess.

"Wednesday! Over here! By the skeleton!" came a

hissing whisper, and Joel slowly rose up out of the shadows.

"Oh, good," Wednesday whispered. She tiptoed over to Joel. "I need to ask you something."

Joel's glasses gleamed in the moonlight. "What?" he asked.

Wednesday fixed him with a solemn gaze. "Do you believe in absolute evil?" she asked.

"Sure," said Joel with a shudder. "Did you meet my mom?"

Wednesday sighed with relief. Joel would understand what she was about to say.

She picked up one of the skeleton's hands and idly swung it back and forth while she talked.

"My uncle Fester is about to get married," she said in disgust. "To this woman in a white uniform."

"A radiologist?" Joel asked, puzzled.

Wednesday shook her head. "A nanny. My stupid little brother's stupid beautiful blond nanny. But I have to go to the wedding anyway. I'm a flower girl. I have a pass from camp." She took a deep breath. "Do you want to come along?"

Joel picked up the skeleton's other hand. "You mean like . . . on a date?" he asked slowly.

Wednesday's voice was firm. "No."

"I'd love to," said Joel without hesitation. "When do—"

"Hello? Is someone there?"

Wednesday and Joel froze in panic. It was Gary!

"Quick!" Wednesday hissed. "Over here!"

When Gary and Becky switched on the lights, all they saw were two bodies stretched out motionless on tables and covered with sheets.

"Who are they?" Becky asked, pointing.

"Must be the Morrison twins," said Gary said casually. "From this afternoon."

"Oh, of course. Bungee jumping?"

Gary shook his head. "Square dancing," he corrected her as he switched off the light again.

It was the night before the wedding, and Debbie was all a-twitter with bridal nerves—that is, if "bridal nerves" means "the icy calm of the practiced serial killer." When she was sure everyone had gone to sleep, she stole into Fester's room.

Fester was lying in bed staring dreamily at the ceiling. "Hello, darling," he said.

"Fester! I thought you were asleep!" Debbie sighed with irritation. "Well, shut your eyes now, sweetheart," she said, forcing a giggle. "It's bad luck to see the bride before the wedding, you know!"

As soon as her fiancé had obeyed, Debbie pulled a tape measure from her pocket and began measuring Fester's neck with it. "Just checking something, babycakes," she said.

She needed his neck size to know whether it would be possible to strangle him with her bare hands.

"Muffin, we're going to be so happy, aren't we?" asked Fester blissfully.

"Of course we are!" Now Debbie was pretending to stab Fester with a dagger. Just in case that's the way I want to do it, she thought. Got to leave my options open.

"You remember your little promise, honey?" she reminded her fiancé.

Fester sighed. "Yes, Debbie. After we're married, I can never see my family again."

Debbie nodded with satisfaction as she mimed chopping off Fester's head. "That's right, darling. Good boy!"

"Remind me why I can't see them, Deb?" Fester sounded a little lost.

Debbie rolled her eyes exasperatedly. "Hon, we've *talked* about this. I just don't feel I can share you with others. My love for you is too . . . too deep. Too rich. Too *blessed* to mess up with other people's love. Can't you see that?"

"I guess so. But I sure wish I could open my eyes and see your beautiful face, too," Fester said plaintively.

"Oh, no, pumpkin, you mustn't! But, Fester, I do have one more request." Debbie pumped several hundred gallons of cuteness into her voice. "I know it's silly . . ."

"Anything! *Anything!*" her fiancé promised her. His eyes were still squinched tight shut.

"I need your signature," Debbie said shyly. "In my wedding album. It's a bridal tradition, you know."

"Oh, I know a great poem for autograph books!" exclaimed Fester. "It starts out 'Put the noose around your neck before we meet again—'"

"I don't need a poem, sweetie," said Debbie

through clenched teeth. "Just your signature is perfect. And don't write any of those U R 4 ME things, either. I love your name all by itself."

She handed Fester a pen. "Eyes shut!" she reminded him.

Fester patted the bed around him. "Where's the autograph book?" he asked.

"Here, I'll help you," said Debbie. She picked up his hand and helped him sign his name in big bold letters at the bottom of the piece of paper.

LAST WILL AND TESTAMENT, read the paper. DEBBIE GETS EVERYTHING.

Morticia's decorator had done a wonderful job. The Addams family grounds were festooned with dead branches and black crepe. And everyone agreed that it was a perfect night for a wedding. Cloudy, dark, and overcast, with the stench of opened graves perfuming the air. Which made sense, because the wedding was being held in the Addams family cemetery.

"I'm so nervous!" Debbie whispered to Morticia as the guests began picking out tombstones to sit on. I hope I can pull this off, she was thinking.

Morticia pressed her hand. "Don't be nervous," she said softly. "You look lovely. As pale as a corpse. Though I do wish we could have persuaded you to buy a black wedding dress instead of that dreadful white thing."

"I feel more traditional in white," Debbie told her. "And I'll have plenty of time to wear black after we're married." When I'm a young, lovely widow.

"Doesn't Wednesday look adorable?" Morticia asked.

Debbie gave Wednesday a quick glance. "Sure," she said with a shrug.

Actually, what Wednesday really looked like was a seriously depressed human being. As Lurch struck up the wedding music, Wednesday dragged herself down the aisle dropping rocks from her black-ribboned basket. The only time she brightened was when she passed the tombstone where Joel was sitting. Their eyes met, and Joel gave her a reassuring grin.

Pugsley was right behind his sister. He was the ring bearer. On his satin pillow sat Thing, who was the secondary ring bearer. Both wedding rings were jammed onto Thing's fingers so it wouldn't lose them.

The ceremony was about to begin. At the back of the cemetery, Debbie checked her watch.

"In ten more minutes," she whispered to herself, "I'll be a wealthy wife."

As she started down the aisle, she could almost feel herself getting richer.

It was an Addams tradition to have Cousin It perform wedding ceremonies. The hairy little creature spoke so clearly that it was a pleasure to listen to him. And his wedding sermons were very inspiring.

"Oooot oot glipper," he began solemnly. He nodded at Fester. "Ooot oot," he repeated. He turned to Debbie, and added, "Gleep glip."

Fester turned to Debbie. He was shaking with emotion, and flecks of spit kept flying out of his mouth as he spoke.

"I, Fester Addams," he declared throbbingly, "do hereby declare my unending love. Debbie, I will worship you forever. I will devote my every waking moment to your happiness. I am your eternal slave!"

Debbie forced back a yawn. "Nice," she said with boredom. "Me too. *Let's keep this thing moving,*" she whispered to Cousin It.

"Gleep glapper glit," said It quickly. That meant "I now pronounce you husband and wife."

Everyone burst into applause except for Cousin Delbert Addams, whose flippers always got stuck together when he clapped.

"Way to go," said Debbie, without enthusiasm. She leaned forward to kiss her new husband, but Fester gestured toward Cousin It. "Kiss It first," he whispered. "Old family custom."

With a shudder, Debbie leaned forward and kissed It on the place she guessed was its cheek.

"Gleep gleep gleep!" It squealed happily.

Debbie tried to smile, but it was hard. One of It's long, long hairs was stuck between her teeth.

Oh, well, she thought as she began yanking out the hair hand over hand. I won't let it bother me. I'm married now.

"You're going to have a wonderful life together," Gomez told her. His face was purple with happiness.

Debbie nodded. "Yes," she answered simply. "Yes, I am."

CHAPTER EIGHT

FESTER IS MISSING!

*A*ddams residence?" asked the moving man.

Gomez nodded, staring out at the huge moving truck parked by the front curb. "That's right, sir. What can I do for you?"

"We're here to pick up all his stuff," said the moving man. He beckoned over his shoulder, and a second moving man walked up to join him. Together they made a rather threatening couple. Even Lurch, who had opened the door for them, fell back a few paces.

"All whose stuff?" asked Gomez.

"Fester Addams's," the second moving man said. "He wants it all outta here."

Morticia gasped. "You must be mistaken! This is Fester's home!"

The men shrugged. "We got a list," the first man pointed out. He pulled a crumpled sheet of paper from his pocket.

"Paper clip collection," he read. "Underwear, one pair. Box of dirt."

Just then Granny walked by the front door carrying a box of dirt. The first man reached out and grabbed it right out of her hands.

"My dirt!" gasped Granny. "What are you doing?"

"Our job, ma'am," said the second moving man. He shoved Gomez and Morticia aside and strode into the house.

"Mail call!" shouted Becky Granger happily. "Pugsley, Wednesday—here's a postcard for you." She held the card just out of Wednesday's reach and read it aloud in a nice, clear voice so everyone in the rec hall could hear.

> Dear Wednesday and Pugsley,
>   I love you dearly, but I can never see you again. When you are grown up, and very lonely, you will understand. Please hate me.
>   Love,
>   Uncle Fester

"That's terrible!" cried Joel.

"Don't judge," Gary Granger reproved him. He snatched the postcard from his wife and scanned it quickly. "Maybe Wednesday and Pugsley have done something to deserve it."

With a Herculean effort, Gomez beats Thing in an arm-wrestling match.

The Addams cemetery offers a playground of sorts for Pugsley and Wednesday

Baby Pubert is a handful — and a mouthful — for Gomez.

Granny finds it easy to knit clothes for the new baby:
Unlike some Addams family members, Pubert needs only two sleeves.

Pugsley and Wednesday plan an experiment in gravity with a cannonball and baby Pubert.

While leaning out the bedroom window to check for rain, Gomez discovers something else falling from above!

Like father, like son . . . Gomez and Pugsley enjoy nature together at Camp Chippewa.

Fester falls heels over head in love with Debbie.

Fester loves bread sticks

...ebbie discover a romantic spot outside the Addan...

Morticia and Gomez attend the wedding — not as festive an occasion as a funeral is for the Addamses.

As always at an Addams wedding, Lurch plays a gloomy melody on the organ.

Till death do us part? Cousin It gives his blessing to the most indescribable couple—Fester and Debbie.

Thing is handy with the shampoo.

Fester will go to any lengths to please his new bride.

Beauty is relative in the Addams family with Cousin Margaret and baby What, Morticia, Gomez, Fester, Dementia, and Wednesday.

"No, we haven't!" said Wednesday. "Something's wrong! We have to help him!"

"You sure do!" said Becky excitedly. "Your uncle sounds as though he's going through a depression. Maybe even a breakdown. You know what he needs?"

"A gym excuse?" suggested Joel.

"No, silly!" said Becky. "A lanyard!"

"A lanyard with a whistle attached!" agreed Gary. "And guess what we're making in Arts and Crafts this afternoon?"

If the members of his family were confused, Uncle Fester wasn't much better off himself. His bewilderment started when he and Debbie returned from their Hawaiian honeymoon. As they stepped off the plane, a uniformed driver walked up to them.

"Afternoon, Mrs. Addams," he said, touching his cap. "Your hearse is here, ma'am. Where's the body?"

Debbie pointed to her new husband. "He's right there."

"But he's alive!" the driver protested.

Debbie's lips were a thin line of exasperation. "Tell me about it," she said crossly.

Now, Fester wondered, what had all that been about?

And where had their new car—a gleaming Lincoln Continental—come from?

Fester asked Debbie that same question on the second day after their return.

"I bought it, silly!" said Debbie. "On our charge card!"

"But it's so . . . new," Fester said confusedly. "So . . . white."

"Bone, not white," Debbie snapped. "I like it."

"Then I *love* it!" said Fester, doing his best to be agreeable. He didn't dare ask Debbie why the new car's license plate read, simply, "DEBBIE 1." He was sure there had to be some good reason. And if he asked her too many questions, she might get mad at him.

All of a sudden, it seemed to Fester, Debbie was always mad at him. She made him buy new clothes— bright-colored, fashionable clothes that felt stiff and starchy compared to his old black robes. She made him cover his nice shiny head with a scratchy toupee. ("I can't have people thinking I've married a fishbowl, can I?" she snapped.) She made him buy her a house in the suburbs and fill it with lots of sissified French antiques. Not a coffin to be seen anywhere!

And no matter how hard Fester begged her, Debbie wouldn't let him see his family. Not even when Gomez, Morticia, and Pubert dropped in for a visit one afternoon.

The housekeeper showed them in before Debbie had a chance to stop her. Morticia and Gomez walked through the front hall looking dazed and ill.

"It's so . . . sick-making," Morticia murmured to Gomez. "How can Fester bear it?" She gestured toward a frilly, flowery tablecloth and moaned faintly, covering Pubert's eyes with her hand so he wouldn't have to see it. "Curtains! Floral arrangements! Gomez, where *are* we? What *is* this place?"

"It looks familiar," Gomez replied. "I think I've seen it in my worst nightmares."

"What are you doing here?" came a clipped, angry voice.

Debbie was walking slowly down the huge curved staircase in the middle of the front hall. The Addamses had never seen her expression before. At least, they'd never seen it aimed at them.

"Surprise!" said Gomez, trying to be cheerful.

"We've brought you some housewarming gifts," said Morticia. "A raven in a cage. And a skull. The skull works anywhere."

"Thanks," said Debbie briefly. "You can just drop them in the trash on your way out."

"On our way out? Might we see my brother first?" asked Gomez.

"No," snarled Debbie. "He doesn't want to see you. Any of you. Or *that,* either." She pointed at Pubert.

"But—why?" asked Gomez, clearly stunned.

"You always treated Fester like a child," Debbie said, drawing herself up. She smiled proudly. *"I* treat him like a man."

Gomez ran a frantic hand through his hair. "Let me hear this from his own lips!" he begged.

"His lips are busy," said Debbie. "But I'll check."

She turned and shrieked, "Fester! You wanna talk to these people?"

"No! Go away!" Fester choked out helplessly from somewhere upstairs.

"That is not my brother!" Gomez howled. "What have you done to him?"

"Get outta my house!" Debbie's voice was so coarse they hardly recognized it.

"Debbie, listen," Morticia pleaded. "I beg you. Be kind to Fester. Not cruel like this. Love him. Feed him. Walk him—"

"HIT THE ROAD!" Debbie interrupted. "And if you ever show your faces around here again, we'll have you locked up! For . . . for trying to visit! Right, Fessie?"

Fester's sad whimper of a voice could barely be heard. "Right, Debbie."

"That's DEBRA!" Debbie screamed.

Debbie's mood seemed a little better the next day. Fester found her floating on a pink raft in the house's gigantic swimming pool. She was sipping a diet soda and soaking up the sun.

"Incredible," muttered Fester as he watched her. "She does things no other woman has ever done."

He raised his voice and greeted her timidly. "Um, Snuggles?"

To his relief, Debbie smiled and motioned to the water. "Come on in, darling! It's heated!" she called gaily.

"But I've already told you I can't swim," Fester protested.

Debbie shook a teasing finger at him. "And *I've* told *you* I'll *teach* you. Just jump in!"

"No." Fester shook his head rapidly. His new toupee wobbled back and forth on his head.

"Oh, come on, honey," Debbie coaxed him. "It's

like with babies. Swimming is a natural instinct. Toss babies into the water and they float. Like croutons in soup!"

Fester bit his lip. "But . . . but what if they don't?"

His wife shrugged. "The pool man takes care of it."

"Well, maybe later," Fester said doubtfully, and turned to go.

"Fester . . ." Debbie called flirtatiously. "I'm lonely."

Fester stopped in his tracks. "You are?"

"Uh-huh," Debbie cooed. "I'm all alone, out on this great big raft. Wouldn't you like to keep me company?"

"I sure would," said Fester eagerly.

"Then *jump!*"

Fester couldn't resist her any longer. He pinched his nose shut and jumped into the pool.

And instantly sank.

With a huge effort he clawed his way to the surface. "Help me! Help!" he screamed.

"Swim!" Debbie told him.

"I can't! *Help!*"

Debbie shrugged. "It was just a theory. I guess I was wrong."

There was a terrible thrashing from the deep end of the pool. Splashes. Screams. More splashes.

Then a bubbling sound. *"Blip. Blip. Blip."*

And then—nothing.

Fester's toupee floated slowly to the surface of the water.

The pool was calm again, and the backyard was silent except for the birds in the trees.

Debbie leaned back in her raft and took a long sip of her soda. Then she picked up her portable phone and punched nine one one.

"Hello?" she purred into the receiver. "You'd better get over here. I seem to be a rich widow all of a—"

With a roar, Fester suddenly burst up out of the water and hurled himself onto the raft. Debbie let out a scream, and it was not a scream of joy.

"It worked! It worked!" Fester babbled. "I can swim! Like a baby!"

Debbie's mouth opened and shut a few times, but nothing came out.

"Why did I ever doubt you?" Fester went on. "I *love* you, Debbie Addams!"

He picked up her hand and covered it with kisses.

Debbie sighed peevishly and slammed down the portable phone.

Back at the Addams mansion, Granny shrieked.

"She's up in the nursery!" Morticia gasped. She and Gomez dashed up the stairs to see what was wrong.

"Stay back!" warned Granny. She was staring into the cradle, her face white with horror.

Neither parent listened to her, of course. Gomez and Morticia raced to the cradle. Panting, they stared inside.

"Oh, no!" Gomez screamed.

"Not this!" Morticia moaned, clutching the side of the cradle. "My baby! My *baby!*"

Pubert was lying happily in the cradle, cuddled into a set of Muppet sheets. His unearthly pallor was gone; his cheeks were pink and healthy looking. His tiny mustache had disappeared. Worst of all, his sleek black hair was now a lovely tangle of golden ringlets.

"What can the matter be?" Gomez asked in a broken voice.

"He's possessed," Granny said grimly. "I looked it up." She pulled a dusty old book out from under the cradle and flipped through its yellowed, cracking pages. "Here we are. 'Infant Possession. Warning signs: severe changes in appearance and personality. Such changes can become permanent.'"

"Permanent?" Morticia could hardly get the word out. "Those golden curls? Those rosy cheeks? That—that *smile?*"

Granny nodded and kept on reading. "'These terrifying changes are most often the result of a troubled family life. They are brought on by separations—'"

"Separations!" Gomez interrupted. *"Fester!"*

"Bingo!" Granny replied. "Pubert knows that something's not right around here. And unless Fester comes back, we're talking dimples."

"Never!" Gomez bellowed. "Not in this house!"

"It's worse than that," Granny whispered. "If things don't change, Pubert might even grow up to be—"

"Don't say it!" Morticia warned.

"—President."

Gomez and Morticia fainted dead away.

CHAPTER NINE

THANKSGIVING
IN
JULY

If Wednesday and Pugsley had known something was wrong at home, they wouldn't have had time to think about it. After Uncle Fester's wedding, they had headed straight back to camp. And now the Camp Chippewa Jamboree had them—and everyone else— in a stranglehold.

After all, it wasn't every day that a summer camp presented a play based on the story of the first Thanksgiving. It wasn't every day that Amanda Buckman was chosen to play little Sarah Miller, the Pilgrim girl who was the lead in the play. And it certainly wasn't every day that Wednesday Addams was chosen to be Pocahontas.

Wednesday could not have been more unhappy when Gary made the announcement.

"I can't do it," she said instantly. "I'm not right for the part."

"Why not?" asked Gary. "The Indians were outcasts on Thanksgiving Day, sort of. You're an outcast here at camp. Plus, you're a brunette, and you have braids. You're perfect for the role! I don't want to hear anything more about it."

And he didn't—until the day of the dress rehearsal.

Everyone was racing around the stage. Becky was supervising the costume fittings and trying to squeeze one especially round little camper into a pumpkin-pie costume. Gary was teaching a song called "Happy Turkey Day" to another group of campers.

"A turkey ran away," he sang, "before Thanksgiving Day. 'I fear,' said he, 'I'd roasted be, if I should stay.'—Yes, Tina?" (A third-grader had just raised her hand.)

"Gary, why do they call the song '*Happy* Turkey Day' if the turkey is so scared that he's running away?"

"Oh, I don't know," said Gary offhandedly. "Maybe later some people caught him and ate him. Now, let's all sing!"

In the midst of all the commotion, one person was absolutely still. That was Amanda Buckman. She was admiring her costume in front of the mirror. And her reflection was so perfect that she couldn't move a muscle.

But she did turn around when she heard Becky screaming at Wednesday. Amanda always liked to watch Wednesday get in trouble.

"Young lady, do you know what time it is?" Becky was yelling. "You are late for your fittings!"

"I don't want to be in the pageant," Wednesday said calmly.

The stage fell silent.

"You don't want to help me realize my vision?" Gary asked.

Wednesday shook her head. "Your work is puerile and underdramatized," she announced. "You lack any sense of structure, character, or the Aristotelian unities."

"Yeah!" Pugsley added loyally.

Gary folded his arms and glared at Wednesday. "Young lady, I am getting just a tad tired of your attitude problem. And that of your cohorts, Pugsley and Joel. You have never quite latched on to the Chippewa spirit." He turned to the other campers. "Isn't that sad?"

"YES!" they shouted in reply.

"Don't we just *hate* that?" Becky joined in.

"YES!"

"Don't we wish they would just *die?*" she went on.

"YEEEEEEESSSSSSSSS!"

"No, we don't," Becky corrected them. "But you know what we're going to do with them? We're going to make an example! We're going to show that anyone, no matter how odd, or pale, or chubby, can still have a darn good time! Whether they like it or not!"

"What are you going to do?" Joel asked apprehensively.

Gary's voice was dark. "You'll see."

Half an hour later, the three misfits were back in their least-favorite place—Harmony Hut. This time around, things were even worse. Gary and Becky had parked the kids in front of a large television set. Now they were trying to decide which video Wednesday, Pugsley, and Joel should watch.

"Yes, indeedy," said Gary evilly. "Just the ticket." He held up a cassette of "Bambi."

"Or this?" Becky held up "Lassie Come Home."

"Or 'The Little Mermaid,'" Gary suggested.

"Stop it!" Wednesday begged. "Please stop!"

"Pugsley's only a child!" Joel said.

Gary paid no attention. He just smiled—and loaded the first cassette into the VCR.

Much later, he and Becky unlocked the door of Harmony Hut. Wednesday, Pugsley, and Joel stared blearily up at them, exhausted. Eight hours of sweetness-and-light videos had turned them into hollow-eyed zombies.

"Good evening," Gary said cordially. "Is there anything you'd like to say?"

"Yes," Wednesday replied. "I'm not perky. But I want to be."

"You do?" Gary squinted suspiciously at her.

"I do," said Wednesday fervently. "I want to smile and sing and dance and be Pocahontas."

Becky let out a little squeal of joy. "Darling, do you really mean it?"

Very slowly, for the first time in her life, Wednesday began to smile. It was a terrifying sight.

* * *

Finally—finally—it was time for the play. The outdoor theater was filled with proud parents. The outhouses were filled with stage-frightened campers. Amanda Buckman's hair was filled with styling gel.

Gary and Becky stood in the middle of the stage, sharing a microphone. To mark the occasion, he was wearing a Pilgrim hat; she was wearing a feathered headband. Both of them were beaming with joy. This was a big, big day for them.

Gary stepped up to the microphone. "Welcome, Chippewa parents and friends! What a splendid turnout! I've been told that every last mom and dad is right here—with the exception of Gomez and Morticia Addams, who are at home with a sick baby."

"What a shame," Becky sighed.

"Selfish," Gary corrected her. "Now. As most of you know, each summer we take this occasion to present an important event in American history. In years past, we have presented stirring musical dramatizations of the Battle of Gettysburg, the signing of the Declaration of Independence, the Johnny Carson farewell."

"But this year," said Becky, "we depict perhaps the most important day in our shared past—the first Thanksgiving."

"A day for *maize,* the Native American word for corn," said Gary. "A day for a terrific turkey dinner and brotherhood. So, white meat and dark meat—take it away!"

The curtains parted. Gary and Becky moved hastily to the prompter's box. A group of campers dressed as turkeys, pumpkins, and ears of corn walked onto the stage and began to sing a song Gary had composed.

> Eat us, Pilgrims and Indians!
> Eat us! Grab your knives and forks!
> Eat us on Thanksgiving Day!

In the prompter's box, Gary smiled with satisfaction. It's not Shakespeare, he thought, but still it's very, very moving.

At the same time, far away, Debbie Jellinsky—now Debbie Addams—was standing in line at a passport office.

"I'd like to renew my passport, please," she said when she finally reached the passport window. "I'll be leaving the country shortly."

"Very good," said the clerk. "Will you be traveling alone?"

"Yes," said Debbie firmly. "I'll be a widow."

As she drove home from the passport office, Debbie rehearsed the lines she planned to be saying very soon.

"Thank you so much. It was a senseless tragedy."

Back at the pageant, Amanda Buckman was in her glory.

"I am so glad we have invited the Chippewas to join us for this holiday meal," she said to the rest of the

Pilgrims. "Remember, these savages are our guests. We must not be surprised at any of their strange customs."

In the audience, Mrs. Buckman dabbed proudly at her eyes.

"After all," Amanda went on, "they have not had our advantages. Advantages such as fine schools. Libraries full of books. Shampoo."

"Shampoo" was Wednesday's cue. She and Joel trooped onstage and marched up to Amanda.

"How," said Wednesday solemnly. "I am Pocahontas, a Chippewa maiden."

"And I am Running Bear, betrothed to Pocahontas," said Joel. "In the play," he added quickly.

"We have brought a special gift for this holiday feast," continued Wednesday. And Pugsley walked onstage in a turkey costume.

"I am a turkey," he announced unnecessarily. "Kill me."

In the prompter's box, Becky clutched Gary's arm excitedly. "This is so *beautiful!*" she murmured.

There were tears in Gary's eyes. "Yes, it is," he replied.

"What a thoughtful gift," Amanda was saying. "Why, you are as civilized as we! Except we wear shoes and have last names. Welcome to our table, our new primitive friends!"

"Thank you, Sarah Miller," Wednesday replied. "You are the most beautiful person I have ever seen. Your hair is the color of the sun, your skin is like fresh milk, and everyone loves you. But we cannot break bread with you."

"What?" blurted Amanda, startled. Wednesday's last line hadn't been in the script. "You can't?" She darted a nervous glance toward the prompter's box. "Becky?"

But Wednesday kept going. "You have taken the land that is rightfully ours," she told Amanda. "Years from now, my people will be forced to live on reservations. The gods of my tribe have spoken. They have said, *Do not trust the Pilgrims. Especially Sarah Miller.*"

Joel began to pound his drum—slowly at first, then faster and faster. There were murmurs of confusion from the audience.

"And for all these reasons," Wednesday said, "I have decided to scalp you and burn your village to the ground."

With wild war whoops, she, Joel, and Pugsley began to shoot flaming arrows around the stage. In an instant the stage was ablaze. The Indians pulled out their papier-mâché tomahawks and began chopping at the Pilgrims. The Pilgrims ran screaming offstage— all except Amanda. She was too confused to move. This gave the Indians the chance to tie her up and shoot her with a bunch of suction-cup arrows.

"Children! CAMPERS!" Becky shrieked from the prompter's box.

"Stop it!" Gary wailed. "You're destroying my text!"

Actually, they were destroying more than that. Hours later, Camp Chippewa was still blazing.

Pugsley had gone to "borrow" one of the camp vans. He had never driven before, but he was pretty sure he could figure it out.

Wednesday and Joel were alone at the boundary fence around the camp. Joel had already cut the barbed wire. He was standing inside the fence; Wednesday was standing outside.

"Can't you come with us?" Wednesday begged.

Joel shook his head. "I have to go back, Wednesday. For the others."

"You're very brave," said Wednesday, impressed.

"Well, I also want to watch the place burn," Joel admitted. "You go. See what's the matter with your baby brother. I hope it's not fatal. Or I hope it is, depending on what you want."

But Wednesday couldn't bring herself to find the van yet. "Joel, I may never see you again," she said. "There are forces tearing us apart. Gary . . . Debbie . . . seventh grade . . ."

Joel swallowed. "I'll never forget you," he said. "You're too weird."

"We'll always have tonight," Wednesday whispered. "And Chippewa."

"Oh—and also this!" Joel said, pulling something out of his pocket. It was a weird-looking object made of plastic and metal.

"What's *that?*" Wednesday asked.

76

Joel smiled. "Amanda's retainer."

He reached over the fence and handed the retainer to Wednesday. For a second the two of them stood there, looking deep into each other's eyes. Then, shyly, they leaned forward and kissed each other.

After that, as one, they wiped their mouths to get rid of the cooties.

CHAPTER TEN

GETTING RID OF FESTER

*I*t was almost suppertime in the Addams-Jellinsky household. Almost suppertime on the three-week anniversary of Debbie's and Fester's wedding. An important time in any couple's marriage, and Debbie was planning to celebrate in a very special way—by getting rid of her husband.

She was giving Fester a bomb for an anniversary present. It was beautifully wrapped and set to go off at six-thirty in the evening. Naturally Debbie had no plans to be around then.

She was up in her bedroom now, putting on her best about-to-be-widowed outfit. Downstairs, Fester was bustling around in the kitchen making an anniversary dinner. When she had finished dressing, Debbie stepped into the kitchen with his present.

"Angel, I'm going out for just a minute," she said. "Dopey me—I forgot the champagne."

"I'll go," Fester offered.

"No!" Debbie barked. "I mean, no," she said more gently. "You're working hard enough. I'll do it. Now, I'm going to leave your present on the table. Don't peek!"

Fester clasped his hands together excitedly. "Oh, please, please, please tell me what it is," he said, just like a little boy. "What is it? Is it string?"

"You never kno-ow . . ." Debbie said teasingly.

"Is it a dog toy?"

Debbie shook a playful finger at him. "Just you wait!" she told him, and turned to leave the kitchen.

"Is it a bomb?"

"What?" Debbie whirled around and stared at him.

Fester kicked the ground sheepishly. "I know what you're going to say," he mumbled. "Wait for my birthday if I want a bomb."

Debbie relaxed again. "That's right, honey," she said. "Now, do you have my little list of things to do?"

"Right here!" With a flourish Fester pulled the list from the pocket of his frilly apron.

"'Cook dinner,'" he read aloud. "'Seal all doors and windows. Turn on all the gas jets. Wait for Debbie.' Yup, I think I can handle that!"

"Oh, Fester," said Debbie softly. "Let me just look at you." She put her hands on his shoulders and stared

79

up into his face. "I always want to remember you just this way."

"What d'you mean?" asked Fester.

"Rich," said Debbie. "Will you miss me?"

Now Fester looked even more mixed up. "Yes, but—but you'll be right back, won't you?"

"Of course I will."

Debbie picked up three huge suitcases and staggered out the front door.

Fester sighed longingly as he watched her car pull out of the driveway. Every time she went away, she took a piece of him with her—a finger, maybe, or an earlobe. He just wasn't complete without Debbie.

But at least her errand would give him time to set the table.

Of course, Debbie wasn't really planning to buy champagne. She was going to use this special time to rehearse what she would say to the police when she got home.

"Darling? *Darling?* DARLING!" she shrieked, eyeing her reflection in the rearview mirror. "My darling husband is gone!"

Too sappy, maybe? Debbie tried another approach.

"He was a wonderful man," she said in a voice of tearful dignity. "I'll always miss . . . uh . . . what's-his-name. *Fester,*" she remembered at last.

Maybe that approach was too dangerous. For some reason people always expected you to remember your husband's name.

What should she say when she got back? What?

Debbie checked her reflection again, trying to make her chin shake.

"But, Officer," she quavered, "m-my husband was *in* the house!"

Perfect. *Perfect.*

Debbie laughed uproariously as she drove along. Then she broke off abruptly and checked the car clock.

Six-twenty. Just about time to head home.

She couldn't wait to see what she would find there.

Just as Debbie pulled up to her driveway, her house exploded.

Instantly the whole building was consumed in flames. A geyser of debris shot up and showered yards for blocks around. Black billowing smoke rose fifty feet into the sky. Out back, the swimming pool began to boil.

"Good timing," Debbie congratulated herself. Quickly she reapplied her makeup. (This was the kind of accident where reporters sometimes showed up.) Then she got out of the car, leaving the motor running in case she needed to make a quick getaway.

"Help. Help," she called calmly. "Someone help. Please won't someone— Oh, my God!"

That last part wasn't rehearsed. It was spontaneous.

Fester had just stepped out of the flaming rubble that was all that was left of the house. He was carrying the roast on a platter. It was cooked to perfection.

"Hi, sweetheart," he called out cheerfully as he walked toward her. "Did you get the champagne?"

"I can't take it anymore," Debbie growled. "I've had it with you!"

Quick as lightning she pulled a revolver out of her purse. "I've been patient enough, Fester," she said. "Now freeze!"

Fester stopped in his tracks. The platter clattered to the ground, and the roast bounced away. "Pookie?" Fester said wonderingly.

Debbie's face was a crazed mask of hatred. "Who are you?" she asked. *"What* are you?"

"I'm your husband!" Fester wailed.

Debbie paid no attention. "I tried to make it look like an accident! I tried to give you some dignity— but, oh, no! Not you! You didn't *want* dignity!"

Fester took a step backward. "What are you saying?" he asked in a trembling voice.

"I'm saying that our marriage is a ridiculous sham!" snapped Debbie. "I'm saying that I want you dead, and I want your money!"

Fester looked as though she had kicked him in the stomach. "But don't you love me?" he asked.

Debbie stared at him incredulously. Then she burst into peals of maniacal laughter.

"Is that . . . a no?" asked Fester forlornly.

"Do I love you?" Debbie wiped away tears of mirth. "Look at yourself! You're a nightmare in a cheap toupee! No woman in her right mind could love you! Does that answer your question?"

And she pointed the revolver straight between his eyes.

Just as she was about to pull the trigger, her car

barreled down on her and knocked her into a flowerbed.

"What the—" Debbie began, struggling to her knees. Then she saw the disembodied hand clutching the steering wheel of her car, and let out a scream of rage.

Fester saw it, too. "Thing!" he called joyfully. "You rescued me!"

He jumped into the car, which slammed into reverse and took off down the driveway.

Debbie was still kneeling in the flowerbed. She took a furious shot at the car as it peeled away—but she missed. Helpless, she watched the car pull away from view.

"I'll get you," she said angrily. "And your little hand, too!"

Morticia was listlessly reading *The Cat in the Hat* to a giggling Pubert when Fester burst into the nursery. "I'm back! Thing rescued me! Can you ever forgive me?" he shouted. "Hey, what's the matter with the baby? He looks horrible! Disgusting! Why are you reading him that garbage? Is he sick?"

"Heartsick! He's missed you!" Morticia said, jumping to her feet. "Oh, Fester! It's wonderful to see you again!"

Now Gomez, Granny, and Lurch came thundering into the room. At the sight of his brother, Fester froze.

"Can you ever forgive me, Gomez?" he asked. "I've

tried to be someone I'm not. Someone terrible. Someone wrong. Someone clean. I live in shame—and the suburbs. And worst of all . . ." His voice trailed off in shame.

"What?" asked Gomez.

Fester could hardly speak. "I sent the children to *camp!*"

At that exact moment Wednesday and Pugsley raced into the room. "Uncle Fester!" Pugsley shouted joyfully. "You're back!"

"Children!" Fester shouted equally joyfully. *"You're* back!"

Pugsley rushed into his uncle's arms, but Wednesday fixed Fester with a steely stare. "You sent us to camp," she reminded him.

"I know, I know," said Fester remorsefully. "I'm an animal."

"They made us *sing,"* Wednesday went on.

Fester couldn't reply. He stood there in silence, his bald head bent low.

At last Wednesday sighed and put her arms around him. "We paid them back," she confessed.

Fester's body sagged with relief. "My own dear family," he said, looking tearfully around the room. "How I've missed you all!"

Morticia had never looked happier. "Oh, Gomez. Our family, together at last," she said. "Three generations . . . all above ground. Isn't it—"

"Hello, in-laws," came an icy voice from behind her. "Mind if I join you?"

Everyone turned toward the door, and Fester let out a whoop of horror.

Debbie was standing there. Fully armed.

In her hands was a submachine gun. Around her neck were wreaths and wreaths of bullets. And on her face was an expression that made it clear this was more than just a social call.

CHAPTER ELEVEN

ALL TOGETHER AGAIN

*D*ebbie's eyes were wide blue pools of innocence.

"I don't want to hurt anybody," she said sweetly. Considering the machine gun in her hands, that was a little hard to believe, but none of the Addamses tried to argue with her.

They weren't in much of a position to argue, anyway. Debbie had strapped them into a row of electric chairs—all of them except the baby. She didn't have a chair small enough for Pubert.

On the other hand, Debbie *had* come up with a way to take care of Thing. She had wrapped him in electrical tape and clipped him to some jumper cables attached to a car battery on the floor. Thing had driven on her lawn, and Debbie wanted revenge.

"It's not my fault," Debbie went on. "You understand that, don't you?"

"Of *course* we understand," said Morticia graciously. "You're a serial killer."

"*I* don't understand," argued Pugsley.

"You will when you're older," Wednesday told him. "It's just that—"

"Listen up, people!" Debbie interrupted. "I don't like guns, or bombs. Or electric chairs. But sometimes people just won't listen. Like my parents, for instance!" Now her features were twisted with rage. "All I ever wanted was a Ballerina Barbie. In her pretty pink tutu. Do you know what they got me?"

Debbie's voice rose to a scream. *"Malibu* Barbie! That's not what I wanted! So Mom and Dad had to go."

The Addams family nodded sympathetically. They could understand that.

"They just didn't love me enough," Debbie continued, sniffing. "All I ever wanted was love. Just love." She gave the family a pleading glance. "You took me in and gave me a wedding. Did any of *you* love me? Really love me?"

No one answered her.

"Don't I deserve love? And jewelry?"

She was walking toward the wall now, where she had set up a huge lever. Each electric chair was wired to the lever.

Time was up for the Addams family.

"Debbie, don't do this," Fester begged. "Let them go. Take me and my money. For what I've done, I deserve to die."

"That's too sweet," said Morticia, touched. "We really couldn't let you."

Wednesday's voice was thoughtful, though. "He *did* send us to camp," she reminded her parents.

But Debbie wasn't listening to any of this. Resting her hand on the switch, she turned to the family one last time. "Good-bye, everyone," she said. "Wish me luck."

"GOOD LUCK, DEBBIE!" shouted the Addamses cheerfully.

And Debbie pulled the switch.

There was a horrible buzzing sound. Instantly Debbie rose ten feet off the floor.

A dazzling shower of sparks shot out of the switch.

Then there was silence. Silence, and no more Debbie. Where she'd stood, all that was left was a pile of ashes, earrings, and charge cards.

"Sssss! Gah-boo!" came Pubert's tiny voice. And he crawled out from behind his mother's electric chair.

With his uncle back, Pubert suddenly looked like his own pale, creepy self again. Even his golden curls were gone. His former hair—slicked down and parted in the middle—had returned.

In his clawed hand was a tangle of wires—wires that were all slimy and droolly. Pubert had been chewing on them.

"He must have reversed the current," Gomez said in an awed voice. "It electrocuted Debbie instead of us."

But no one was complaining.

"Here, Pubert," said Wednesday sweetly. "Here's a birthday present. I love you."

She smiled sweetly at Pubert, who was nestled in Pugsley's lap. Then she set down the present—a little pull toy—and began pulling it along the floor.

Pubert wriggled out of his brother's lap and eagerly began to crawl after the toy. A scimitar sliced down from the ceiling, just missing him. Two bowling balls rolled toward each other and crashed together just as he crawled out of range. A massive safe hurtled from above and missed him by a hair. Still he continued crawling steadily, and finally he reached Wednesday.

"Here," she said in disgust. None of her plans to get rid of him had worked. Pubert always managed to survive. "Happy Birthday." Wednesday shoved the pull toy into his hand and walked down the hall.

Nine months had passed since Debbie had zapped herself. The Great Room was festively draped in black, and guests were just starting to arrive for Pubert's first birthday party. Joel was there, dressed as a miniature version of Gomez. ("You look very disturbing," Wednesday complimented him.) Cousin Margaret and Cousin It and their fuzzy new baby, What, were there as well.

And they'd brought their nanny, Dementia—a woman whose head was just as round and bald and shiny as Uncle Fester's. The instant she and Fester caught sight of each other, they both knew: This was real love. Not like Fester's infatuation for a gun-toting maniac who knew how to throw together a row of electric chairs—but the real thing.

"Time to light the cake!" Gomez called to everyone. "Thing, will you do the honors?"

With a flourish, Thing lit the single candle on the moss-colored cake. (It had "Happy First Birthday, Pubert" written on it in black icing.) The Addams family burst into a rousing cackle of "Happy Birthday to You." Then they all watched as Pubert pursed his slimy little lips and blew as hard as he could.

Of course, Pubert was too little to tell anyone what he had wished for. But to judge from the wicked little smile on his face, it was for something dreadful and disgusting.

Just right for the newest member of the Addams family.

ABOUT THE AUTHOR

ANN HODGMAN is a former children's book editor and the author of over twenty-five children's books, including the popular *My Babysitter Is a Vampire* and *Stinky Stanley* series for Minstrel Books. In addition to humorous fiction for children, she has written teen mysteries and nonfiction for reluctant readers. She lives with her husband and two children in Washington, Connecticut.